DC SUPER HERO
FAIRY TALES

BATMAN™
AND THE BEANSTALK

by Sarah Hines Stephens
illustrated by Agnes Garbowska
colors by Sil Brys

BATMAN CREATED BY
BOB KANE WITH BILL FINGER

STONE ARCH BOOKS
a capstone imprint

W9-CRS-896

Published by Stone Arch Books, an imprint of Capstone
1710 Roe Crest Drive, North Mankato, Minnesota 56003
capstonepub.com

Library of Congress Cataloging-in-Publication Data
Names: Hines Stephens, Sarah, author. | Garbowska, Agnes, illustrator.
Title: Batman and the beanstalk / by Sarah Hines Stephens ; illustrated
by Agnes Garbowska.
Description: North Mankato, Minnesota : Stone Arch Books, [2021] |
Series: DC super hero fairy tales | Audience: Ages 8–11 | Audience:
Grades 4–6 | Summary: In this retelling of Jack and the Beanstalk,
Batman climbs a huge vine that has sprung up in Gotham City to
find people in trouble and hulking villain, Solomon Grundy.
Identifiers: LCCN 2021015956 (print) | LCCN 2021015957 (ebook) |
ISBN 9781663910516 (hardcover) | ISBN 9781663921222 (paperback) |
ISBN 9781663910486 (pdf)
Subjects: CYAC: Superheroes—Fiction. | Fairy tales—Adaptations. |
Characters in literature—Fiction.
Classification: LCC PZ7.H574 Bat 2021 (print) | LCC PZ7.H574 (ebook) |
DDC [Fic]—dc23
LC record available at https://lccn.loc.gov/2021015956
LC ebook record available at https://lccn.loc.gov/2021015957

Designed by Hilary Wacholz

Printed and bound in the USA. 004270

TABLE OF CONTENTS

THE WORLD'S GREATEST
SUPER HEROES COLLIDED WITH
THE WORLD'S BEST-KNOWN
FAIRY TALES TO CREATE . . .

DC SUPER HERO
FAIRY TALES

Now, Batman must take down a towering vine that has suddenly sprung up in Gotham City . . . and face the giant foe waiting at the top in this twisted retelling of "Jack and the Beanstalk"!

CHAPTER 1

A Growing Concern

One dark and cloudy evening, billionaire Bruce Wayne sat in his mansion overlooking Gotham City. He was paging through the daily newspaper. But as Bruce read, his already serious expression grew even more grave.

The news was mysterious.

Soon Bruce's loyal butler, Alfred, came into the room. He immediately noticed his employer's frown.

"Is something troubling you, Master Wayne?" Alfred asked.

"It's curious." Bruce tapped two different articles with his index finger. "There have been two disappearances in Gotham City this week. Gregory Gild went missing, and now so has Mariah Vega."

"Gregory Gild . . . ," Alfred repeated. "Is that the son of Magnus Gild, the wealthy shipping tycoon?"

"The very one," Bruce said. He had met the young heir to the Gild fortune on several occasions. The young man was definitely going places and had a bright future.

"And Mariah Vega . . . what a voice!" Alfred closed his eyes, imagining the sweet voice of the famous opera singer.

Bruce nodded. "Mariah had just arrived in Gotham City. She was supposed to perform last night, but she never took the stage. Her dressing room was empty. Her disappearing so soon after Gild strikes me as strange."

"Did they know one another?" Alfred asked.

"No, that's why it's so odd," Bruce said.

He studied the articles and waited for Alfred to say something more. The butler was wise and often offered good advice. But when Bruce looked up, he saw Alfred had been distracted by something else.

The butler had pulled back the living room curtains to reveal the evening sky. A familiar shape inside a circle of light darkened the clouds. It was the shadow of a bat!

Without a word, Bruce stood and disappeared into the lair that waited below Wayne Manor. It was a place of secrets—secret codes, secret gadgets, secret vehicles, and Bruce Wayne's secret identity. It was there that Bruce Wayne became Batman, the Super Hero.

The Bat-Signal had lit up the sky for only a minute. But in that time, Bruce had put on his suit, cape, and cowl. He was ready to answer the call!

Batman leaped into his Batmobile and sped out of the Batcave through a hidden tunnel. He raced toward Gotham City Police Headquarters. After parking in a back alley, he scaled the tall building and dropped silently onto the flat roof. The man who had turned on the signal was already waiting there. It was Police Commissioner Gordon.

The hero stepped toward the head of police. He was certain they were going to discuss the strange mystery of the two missing people. But the commissioner had something else on his mind.

"Batman! Thank you for coming. Something strange has come up," Gordon said. "A huge vine is growing on the edge of the city. It's like nothing we've ever seen!"

"A vine?" Batman asked. "You called me to talk about *plants*?"

"This is not just any vine," Gordon went on. "It sprung up overnight. Literally. It is several stories tall and still growing. It's not normal. I would like you to take a look at it."

"Right now?" Batman asked. He was still puzzled. "I thought you had called me about the disappearances. About Gild and Vega."

The commissioner shook his head. "Their disappearances are troubling, and we're looking into them," he said. "But this vine is a bigger threat than it sounds like. See it for yourself. Then you will understand why this is a priority."

Without another word, Batman rushed to the Batmobile. It did not take long for him to find the vine.

The plant was exactly where the police commissioner had said it would be. It was growing beside a large marsh on the edge of Gotham City.

It was also true that the plant was unlike anything Batman had ever seen before. He could barely believe his eyes.

What loomed before the hero was beyond tall. It was massive!

The base of the plant was so gigantic it took Batman a minute just to walk around it. It was covered in curling tendrils. It was dripping with heart-shaped leaves the size of sailboat sails.

Squinting up in the dim light, Batman realized the plant looked exactly like a giant beanstalk.

For a long moment, Batman simply gazed up in amazement. The plant grew so high that he could not see the top. It disappeared into the dark clouds overhead.

CREEEAAK!

Batman's head snapped down. Strange sounds were coming from the plant.

CREEEEEAAAAK!

It's the sound of the plant growing! Batman realized.

Suddenly a tendril sprang from the vine. It curled around Batman's leg, throwing him off balance.

WHAM!

The hero fell to the ground.

Batman pulled at the vine on his leg. He tried to snap it in two, but it was no use.

"This is one tough plant," he grunted.

Batman took a Batarang from his Utility Belt and cut himself free. A new shoot appeared almost instantly from where he had made the cut.

RRRUUUMBLE

As Batman got to his feet, he could feel the soil shifting. The beanstalk's roots were growing as fast as the vine above.

Now the Super Hero understood why the commissioner felt this plant posed a threat. At the rate it was growing, the beanstalk would soon push up pavement and topple buildings. A plant like this could take over the city!

There's only one villain I can think of who is capable of making a plant grow so large and so out of control, Batman thought. *And there is only one way to see if my suspicions are correct.*

He had to get to the root of the problem. But in this case, that didn't mean digging down. Batman grabbed the beanstalk and began to climb.

CHAPTER 2

BIGGER PROBLEMS

Moving hand over hand, Batman made his way slowly up the giant beanstalk. Multiple tendrils had woven themselves together. They created a sort of ladder.

But the vine was continuing to twist and grow as the hero climbed. Each handhold and foothold needed to be chosen with care.

Suddenly a fast-growing shoot shifted. Batman's foot slipped! He started to slide down the vine.

With a quick motion, Batman grabbed the grapnel gun from his Utility Belt. Then he fired.

FWOOSH! KER·CHUNK

The hook at the end of the rope dug into the vine.

In an instant, the Dark Knight was swinging back toward the top of the plant. He grabbed the twisting tendrils. He touched another button on his belt.

Short, sharp blades sprang out from the ends of his boots and gauntlets. They pushed into the plant and gave him a better grip.

Batman climbed higher still. Soon, he could not make out the ground below. Then he entered into a thick cloud that made it hard to see anything at all.

The plant grew slippery from the mist, but Batman kicked into the tough stem. His spikes kept him from falling.

At last, the hero came out from the cloud. In the moonlight, he saw that the plant spread out at this height. It formed a massive platform in the sky.

But what grabbed Batman's attention most of all was what stood in the center of the leafy platform. A short distance away, there was a large building made of vines.

It's a perfect lair for a vegetal villain! Batman thought.

Batman made his way silently over the flat leaves. He reached the towering door of the building. It was unlocked.

He stepped in and stopped short.

Like the plant that grew up to it, everything inside the building was huge. Down a hallway, Batman could see a room filled with oversized wooden chairs and a table. The table held a grand meal. It was also set with large platters, goblets, and silverware the size of serving spoons.

Batman walked carefully toward the room. Suddenly a green-gloved hand snatched his shoulder and pulled him back.

The Caped Crusader reacted instantly. He grabbed the hand and flipped the snatcher over his shoulder and onto the floor.

THUD!

Batman stood ready to battle as the attacker sprang back up. The foe turned, and the hero finally saw who it was.

Poison Ivy.

"I thought I would find you here!"
Batman said. "There is only one thumb
green enough to grow this giant mess."

Batman had faced off against Poison Ivy
before. The red-haired Super-Villain was able
to command plants to do her bidding. She
was a dangerous foe. But now, Batman saw
something he had never seen before in her
green eyes: fear.

"What are you up to, Ivy?" Batman asked.

Poison Ivy lowered her fists to put a finger
to her lips. Her eyes darted toward the large
dining room.

"Hello to you too, Batman," Poison Ivy
said. Her voice was a whisper. "I was actually
hoping you would come. Things have gotten
a little . . . out of hand."

A moment later Batman heard for himself why Ivy looked so terrified.

The plant floor shook.

BOOM BOOM BOOM

From the shadowy hall, Batman watched a huge man stomp into the dining room. The giant's back was turned to the hallway as he sat down heavily at the oversized table. He grabbed an empty cup and waved it in the air.

"Ivy!" the man shouted. "I'm thirsty!"

Poison Ivy flinched. She pressed her finger to her lips again.

"Stay quiet and keep out of sight! We need your help!" she whispered to Batman. Then she hurried toward the room and called, "Coming!"

Batman was speechless. Poison Ivy had *never* asked him for help before. She had to be in real trouble!

And why had she said "we" need help? Batman wondered.

He peered out of the darkness, wondering who else might be in this garden lair.

The huge man at the table turned. "Where is my water, Ivy?" he yelled.

Batman quickly pulled back into the shadows. He recognized the thirsty giant. It was the villain Solomon Grundy!

After being left for dead in a swamp and injected with chlorophyll, Solomon Grundy had returned from the beyond part plant and all evil. He was a brute.

Only now, the villain was larger. Much larger. He was at least twice his usual size.

"What has happened to Grundy? What have you been up to, Ivy?" Batman asked in a whisper after Poison Ivy had filled the man's glass and slipped back into the hall.

Poison Ivy shuddered. "I was just trying to grow extra large vines to stop the spread of concrete in Gotham City."

"That doesn't explain *him*," Batman said. He tilted his head toward the table where Grundy was eating noisily.

"I planted my magic beans on the edge of the city. Grundy's marsh just happened to be on the same edge," Poison Ivy said. "He must have seen me planting and eaten one of the beans—he eats everything. Then he started to grow, just like my beanstalk!"

Batman nodded. That explained his size, but . . .

"I climbed up here to get away from him and make myself a garden lair in the sky," Ivy went on. "But Grundy followed me out of his mucky marsh and took over my plant penthouse and—"

"Kept you on as a servant," Batman finished.

"It's so embarrassing. I only wanted to grow a green place to live. I never meant to grow a giant. Now everything is out of control," Ivy said. "I can't get away and all he wants is more, more, more to satisfy his giant appetites! He's even—"

"*IIIIIVVVVYYYY!*" boomed Solomon Grundy from the table.

Ivy hurried to take care of the hungry, growing villain. Batman was left wondering what else she had been going to say.

Grundy emptied his plate as fast as Ivy could fill it. He shoved fistfuls of dinner into his mouth. He ordered his glass to be filled again and again.

While Ivy poured more water into the bucket-sized cup, Batman inched closer to the room. He squinted in the dim light. He thought he saw movement on the other side of the table.

Is it a person? Batman wondered. *Is that what Ivy was going to tell me about?*

Grundy suddenly stopped shoving food into his mouth. He sniffed the air. Then he bellowed a tuneless rhyme that sent chills down Batman's spine:

"Fee-fi-fo-fum. I smell some*one*. Be it man or be it bat, I'll trap him here just like a rat!"

CHAPTER 3

Golden Boy

Batman darted back into the shadows as Solomon Grundy heaved himself up from the table to investigate.

Poison Ivy stepped in front of the entryway to the dining room. She stood directly between the massive man and the hiding hero.

"Oh, Grundy. The only creatures in your lair are the ones you've trapped and brought here yourself!" she said with a forced laugh. "You need to relax. Let me fill your cup."

"*Hmph,*" Grundy muttered, but he sat back down and drained his glass. He pounded his fist on the table and gave a new order.

"Sing!" he roared.

At first Batman thought the huge villain was shouting at Poison Ivy. But then he saw a figure step out from the dark corner and into the light.

It was Mariah Vega, the missing opera star! She trembled in fear before the seated giant.

"Sing!" Grundy shouted again.

Mariah's voice shook as she began to sing. Her beautiful soprano voice filled the space. The music settled like a spell over everything.

Batman and Ivy locked eyes across the room. *Wait*, she mouthed at him.

Batman frowned. It was not easy for the hero to resist the urge to jump in and rescue the frightened singer immediately. Nor was it easy to trust Poison Ivy. He knew she had tricks aplenty up her green sleeves. She had fooled him with her pollens and potions in the past.

But the Dark Knight felt this time was different. Besides, it would be difficult to face giant Solomon Grundy head-on.

So, Batman stayed where he was. Soon, he saw why Ivy wanted him to wait.

As Mariah sang, Grundy became more and more calm. He was like a baby listening to a lullaby. He set down his cup. He stopped stuffing his face. His eyes began to blink and close.

SKRRODONNNK!

A loud snore shook the entire plant palace. Grundy was asleep!

Mariah continued her beautiful song. Standing beside the snoring giant, Poison Ivy motioned to Batman. She jerked her head toward a door in the long hall.

Batman crept closer and silently turned the door's handle. He slipped into the room as Grundy's snores shook the leafy walls.

SKRROOONK! GRAAAHHNK!

The small room was darker than the hallway. It took a moment for Batman's eyes to adjust. When they did, he saw a young man slumped in the corner.

Batman rushed over to confirm what he already knew. It was Gregory Gild, the missing heir!

Batman gently moved Gregory to wake him. The young man's eyes fluttered open.

"Where am I?" he asked.

"You've been kidnapped," Batman replied in a whisper. "I believe you're being held captive by Solomon Grundy."

"The giant," Gregory added. His eyes grew wide as the memory returned. "He wants money from my family!"

Grundy took Gregory to try to get a ransom! Batman realized. *It makes sense. Keeping up with his giant appetite would be expensive. And it seems he has an appetite for fine music too. So he nabbed Mariah to entertain him up here in the clouds.*

"Never mind," Batman told Gregory. "He won't get any money, because I'm going to get you out of here."

The Super Hero helped Gregory to his feet. He was already making plans to grab the opera star too. He would make a run for freedom with *both* of the giant's prisoners.

But Batman quickly realized that running was out of the question. Gregory was still groggy. He could barely stand. There was no way he'd be able to climb down a towering vine. Batman would have to carry Gregory.

The Caped Crusader was going to have to rescue Grundy's captives one at a time.

Batman's motions matched his thinking— quick and quiet. Removing the Batrope from his Utility Belt, he made a sling to carry Gregory on his back.

The pampered young man stared at the sling. "You expect me to ride piggyback?" Gregory scoffed.

Batman silenced him with a look. "It is the only way out of here. Now, don't make a sound," he said. He lifted Gregory onto his back and pulled the rope tight.

Opening the door a crack, Batman peeked into the dining room.

GRRROONNK! PHHHLAFT!

Grundy had fallen face-first into his plate and was now snoring into his mashed potatoes. Mariah Vega was still singing. The terrified woman looked as if she might soon fall over herself.

Poison Ivy stood on the far side of the room. She had been waiting and watching. When she saw Batman with Gregory tied to his shoulders, she began to motion.

Go, Poison Ivy mouthed, waving him away.

Unfortunately, Mariah Vega noticed Ivy's signal too. The singer turned and saw the man dressed all in black like a powerful bat. She wasn't sure if he was there to help or do harm! Her voice cracked.

OOOOOOHHHH! AAAAAAAAH!

Her operatic singing became high-pitched screaming. Grundy began to stir.

There was not a moment to lose! Batman raced for the front door of the green lair. He moved as quickly as he could while carrying the young man on his back.

The Super Hero burst out into the night. As he sped across the leafy platform, Batman listened for Grundy's footsteps. Instead, Mariah's sweet song began drifting through the air once more. Then, like distant thunder, Grundy's snores resumed their rumble.

SKRROOOONNNK!

The giant had fallen back to sleep.

But when he wakes, he'll find his golden boy missing, Batman thought as he made his way down the plant. *Grundy is sure to be furious.*

∽ ∾

"What's all this?" Commissioner Gordon asked when Batman reached the bottom of the beanstalk. "I thought you would be bringing down Poison Ivy! And I was hoping you would bring down this awful plant as well. But . . . is that Gregory Gild?"

The wealthy heir struggled out of the sling on Batman's back. "Yes!" Gregory said, pushing away from the Dark Knight. "Batman rescued me from that . . . beast!"

"Do you mean from Poison Ivy?" the confused commissioner asked.

"No, not from Ivy," Batman replied. "She is up there. And she is the one behind this monster beanstalk, but Poison Ivy is *not* our biggest problem."

The commissioner's eyes grew wide as the Dark Knight filled him in on what he had discovered.

Then suddenly the soil beneath their feet shifted. The plant creaked and shot out fresh tendrils that punched into the concrete. The beanstalk, like the problems overhead, was growing bigger with each passing second!

CHAPTER 4

Back Up the Beanstalk

The next evening, Batman sped back to the beanstalk on his Batcycle. During the day, he and Alfred had worked on a plan to take down the huge weed.

But before they could put it into action, Batman needed to get Mariah Vega safely back on the ground.

As he drove, the Dark Knight saw that he would have to act fast. The huge vine now loomed over the city like a green tower.

The twisted plant was nearly twice the size it had been the day before, and it was still growing!

"I hope Solomon Grundy isn't growing at this rate," Batman said when he met with Commissioner Gordon at the beanstalk.

The commissioner and his officers had been staked out beside the big vine all day. They were making sure that nobody went up or came down.

"Are you sure you don't want any help?" Gordon asked. "We could take a chopper up there."

"Then I'll lose the element of surprise," Batman said. "Besides, I like working alone."

And so, Batman began climbing. He kept his ears peeled as he went. He was hoping to hear Mariah Vega's singing.

A sleeping giant will be much easier to deal with than a raging giant! the Dark Knight thought. But all he heard was the wind.

Everything was still quiet and calm when Batman reached the spot where the leaves stretched out in all directions. The Super Hero crept toward the great green fortress.

He found the front door cracked open. Ivy had clearly been waiting for him to return.

As he slipped inside, Batman heard something echo in the long entry hall. But it was not the sound he had hoped to hear.

"Fee-fi-fo-fief! I smell a bold thief. He stole the heir, the gilded son. And he'll be dust before I'm done!"

Solomon Grundy's voice boomed. The leafy floor shuddered beneath Batman's feet as the giant paced in the dining room.

"You're smelling things that aren't there, Grundy!" Batman heard Poison Ivy say. "You probably just smell dinner. Now come. Sit!"

"If I'm smelling things, then where is Gregory?" Grundy asked.

"How should I know where your golden boy went?" Poison Ivy replied. "I've been busy taking care of you."

Batman slunk down the dark hallway while the villains argued. If Grundy suspected that someone had taken Gregory, getting Mariah out would be even more difficult.

The Dark Knight peered carefully into the dining room to study the situation.

There was Mariah Vega. She stood, terrified, in the corner on the far side of the room. It was right past the oversized table where Solomon Grundy was sitting.

Batman frowned. He would have to sneak by the giant villain to reach the singer!

At least Grundy doesn't appear to be much larger. He's not growing as fast as the beanstalk, the hero realized. *Still, he is big enough!*

Batman watched Poison Ivy fill Grundy's glass and place platters of food on the table. She looked nervous. She also kept sneaking glances in the direction of the hall where Batman was hiding.

Grundy took a swig from his glass. "I tell you, I smell a thief!" he hollered. Then he hurled the cup across the room.

CRAAASSSH!

The glass hit the far wall and shattered.

Batman used the distraction to make his move! He darted into the room and under the table.

Batman crouched low. The extra long, extra large table could hide him as he moved across the room. But he had to be careful. He would be passing right beneath Grundy's nose!

Creeping slowly, Batman moved toward the side of the room where Mariah stood. He was also moving closer to Grundy. Soon Batman was so close that he could hear the giant chewing.

"Maybe it's your food that stinks!" Grundy complained to Poison Ivy with his mouth full. Then, he stopped talking.

SNIFF

Grundy sniffed. Then he sniffed again. It was as if he was taking "tastes" of the air with his big nose.

SNIFF SNIIIIIFF SNUUUUFFF

Batman froze. The huge man shifted in his chair. His hands appeared on his lap as he leaned to peer under the table.

Batman was trapped! There was nowhere to hide!

"How about a song?" Poison Ivy asked loudly.

The giant jerked back upright, and Batman crept farther away.

"Fine," Grundy huffed. "But that thief's stench is still here!"

"I don't smell a thing," Ivy said again. "Now, relax and enjoy your music."

Then, just as she had the night before, Mariah Vega stepped forward. She drew in a deep breath and began to sing. The effect on Solomon Grundy was immediate.

From his hiding place, all Batman could see were Grundy's enormous legs. But that was enough to tell that he was falling under Mariah's spell. The villain's knees relaxed. His legs slumped.

Batman waited. He stayed silent and still beneath the table. At last, he heard the sound he was hoping for.

SKROOOONK!

A snore erupted from Grundy's mouth.

Not a second later, Batman burst out from under the table. He wanted to rescue Mariah and make his getaway before the villain woke up.

But the hero may have acted *too* quickly. When Batman leaped out, all Mariah saw was a black shadow rushing toward her. Once again, her singing turned to screaming!

OOOOOOHHHH! AAAAAAAAH!

"I'm here to help!" Batman told her. "I'm going to get you out of here!"

It was no use. The startled opera singer continued to scream.

Batman had no time to explain and no time to lose. Solomon Grundy had stopped snoring. His eyes were open, and he was staring right at the hero!

CHAPTER 5

TAKE DOWN

Solomon Grundy slammed both fists on the table. The dishes jumped, and his water spilled. He lurched to his feet.

"You!" the giant villain growled, pointing at Batman. "You stole my golden heir! You are a thief and a rat!"

"*You* are a kidnapper and a bully," the Super Hero replied. "And I'm not a rat. I'm a bat."

RRRAAAAAGH!

Grundy yelled with rage. With one hand, he flipped the table loaded with food. The heavy table and its contents hurtled toward Batman and Mariah Vega.

The Dark Knight quickly grabbed the screaming opera singer and dove to the side. Plates shattered and food splattered onto the ground.

With one mighty step, Grundy crossed over the upturned table. He raised a fist, ready to bring it crashing down onto Batman's head.

FWIIIIT! FWIIIIT!

In the blink of an eye, vines shot out of the wall. They wrapped around Grundy's clenched hand! His fist stopped in midair.

The giant stared in confusion at his hand. Then he looked over his shoulder.

Poison Ivy stood nearby with her arms stretched out.

Batman grinned. Although Ivy could not control Grundy, it seemed she could still control her beanstalk.

Unfortunately, the vines were no match for Solomon Grundy's strength. He tore them away like spiderwebs. But it was all the time Batman needed.

The Super Hero grabbed a gas pellet from his Utility Belt. He threw it onto the ground. The pellet exploded instantly, filling the room with dark blue smoke.

With another quick motion, Batman fired his grapnel gun across the room. The hook at the end dug into the ceiling above the exit.

Then, grasping Mariah around the waist, Batman hit the retract button. The grapnel pulled the hero and singer through the blue smoke and right over Solomon Grundy's head.

A huge hand reached up through the thick smoke and closed on . . . nothing! Batman swung around the reaching fingers.

The hero landed easily by the exit. Then he lifted Mariah Vega up and carried her out of the leafy hideout. Batman didn't like leaving Poison Ivy to fend for herself, but he needed to focus on getting Mariah to safety.

The stunned opera singer stopped screaming as soon as they were out the door. But they were not yet out of danger.

BOOM BOOOM BOOOOM

Grundy's footsteps pounded behind them.

Each step grew louder. With his long legs, the giant foe could cover an amazing amount of ground.

Still, Batman was faster. He ran at top speed to the spot where the beanstalk led back down to Gotham City.

"Hold on," Batman told Mariah.

There was no time to make a sling of ropes to hold the opera singer. Instead, Batman quickly set up a jump line. It was the same type he used to slow his fall when dropping from the sides of Gotham City's tall buildings.

"What are you—" Mariah Vega started to ask.

Then the Super Hero leaped.

AAAAAAHHH!

Mariah's powerful lungs let out a scream as the two dropped down the side of the beanstalk. Her arms tightened around Batman's shoulders.

Even with the screaming and the wind whistling in Batman's ears, he could still hear Grundy's stomping overhead. Then the vine started to shake. The giant was climbing down!

Batman could see the ground rushing closer. Police officers were waiting there with a large net stretched out between them.

"Jump!" Batman commanded Mariah.

The singer hesitated for a moment. Then she leaped and bounced safely into the net.

A second later, Batman released the jump line. He dropped to the ground, rolled, and easily came to his feet.

He looked up just in time to see Poison Ivy swinging down on a vine. Somehow, she had gotten out of the green house ahead of Grundy!

"Not so fast," Batman said, grabbing Ivy by the arm when she reached the bottom. "I helped you. Now you need to help fix the problem that you created."

Ivy jerked away. "What do you expect me to do?" she huffed.

"Help me cut this beanstalk down!" Batman said.

SKREEEEE!

Just then, the squeal of tires cut through the air. The Batmobile pulled up right to the base of the beanstalk.

Inside, completely hidden by the dark windows, sat Alfred.

Alfred had driven the Batmobile over, just as the hero and butler had planned earlier in the day. The front of the vehicle was now rigged with a large saw blade. It was the perfect tool for cutting unwanted weeds.

"You know I don't kill plants!" Ivy said, eyeing the blade.

"Just stop the vine from sprouting again as it falls. The Batmobile will make the cut, and I'll make sure that the two giants don't crush anyone," Batman said.

The stalk shook again. A roar came from overhead. Grundy was getting closer!

That was enough to convince Poison Ivy. She gave a sharp nod and got into position.

Batman signaled to Alfred. The Batmobile edged closer toward the plant. The blade on the front began to spin.

ZZZZZRRRRR!

"Look out!" Batman warned the people on the ground. Then the hero quickly jumped onto his waiting Batcycle. He had to keep the beanstalk from falling toward the city!

Using a remote Batarang, the Caped Crusader sent a cable around the huge vine as high up as he could. Then he sped in the opposite direction of Gotham City and the fleeing crowd.

The cable jerked tight. The Batcycle slowed as it pulled against the falling beanstalk. But Batman revved the engine and kept pulling. He tugged the beanstalk away from the city he loved and straight toward Grundy's marsh.

The vine shook. It swayed this way and that like an enormous serpent.

Alfred drove the Batmobile forward. The saw blade continued to slice and cut through the massive plant.

Poison Ivy stood nearby with her eyes closed and arms outstretched. She used every ounce of her powers to keep the vine from sending out new roots.

Then . . .

BOOOOOOM!

The beanstalk toppled, bringing Solomon Grundy down with it.

Waves surged as the plant and giant splashed into the marsh. Batman jumped off his Batcycle and waded in.

The hero found Grundy snoring softly in the mucky water. The fall had stunned the large foe. He would not be getting up anytime soon.

After a signal from Batman, Gordon's team took to the sky in helicopters. Chopper blades whirred overhead. The police dropped a large net to hold Solomon Grundy in place.

Stepping into the shallow water, Commissioner Gordon clapped a hand on the Caped Crusader's shoulder.

"You've done it again, Batman," said the commissioner. "Gild and Vega are safe. We will be taking Grundy in for kidnapping—as soon as we can fit him in a cell. And we'll be burning the beanstalk, too, just to make sure it never sprouts again!"

Batman nodded. His expression was unreadable beneath his cowl.

"I'm just glad I could cut the situation down to size," the hero said.

Just then Gordon's radio crackled to life.

"Sir, we have a problem," an officer reported. "Poison Ivy is—"

"Gone," Batman said at the same time as the officer.

Poison Ivy was as slippery as seaweed and had used the crashing vine as a distraction to make her getaway.

Although the Dark Knight knew he had not seen the last of the green villain, he hoped he had seen the last of her magic beanstalk.

THE ORIGINAL STORY:
JACK AND THE BEANSTALK

Once upon a time, a widow sent her son, Jack, to market to sell their only cow. But Jack traded the cow for magic beans! Furious, Jack's mother tossed the beans out the window.

The next morning, Jack discovered the beans had grown into the sky! He climbed the beanstalk and found a house at the top. A kind woman in the kitchen gave the boy some food. But as Jack ate, a giant stomped into the house! It was the woman's husband. Jack quickly hid. The huge man sniffed the air and said, "Fe-fi-fo-fum. I smell the blood of an Englishman. Be he alive or be he dead, I'll grind his bones to make my bread."

The woman told her husband he was imagining things. Soon, the giant fell asleep while counting his gold. Jack snuck out, snatched a bag of gold, and hurried away.

But curious Jack decided to make another visit. The giant's wife again hid the boy when her husband returned. After a meal, the giant called for his hen that lay golden eggs. As the man dozed off, Jack grabbed the hen and raced off.

Jack climbed the stalk a third time and waited in the house. After eating, the giant called for his magic harp and ordered it to sing. Jack took the treasure right as the man started to snooze. But the harp screamed—and woke the giant!

Jack could hear the giant following him down the plant. He called for his mother to grab an ax. When he reached the ground, Jack used the ax to bring the beanstalk and the giant toppling down, never to get up again.

SUPERPOWERED TWISTS

Jack takes gold coins, a hen that lays golden eggs, and a magic harp from the giant at the top of the beanstalk. Batman rescues a rich heir and famous opera singer from the huge villain's lair.

The fairy tale beanstalk grows from magic beans that Jack got from a mysterious stranger. In this story, the crook Poison Ivy makes and plants the beans that sprout the towering plant!

The giant's kind wife hides Jack so the boy doesn't get eaten. Poison Ivy hides Batman from Solomon Grundy because she needs help taking the big brute down!

Jack's giant and Solomon Grundy both smell intruders hiding in their homes. They recite the line that the fairy tale giant is most famous for: Fe-fi-fo-fum!

Jack's mother brings over an ax when the giant is climbing down. Batman gets help from Alfred, who drives the Batmobile outfitted with a blade that's perfect for cutting through plants.

TALK ABOUT IT

1. As Batman climbed the beanstalk, he expected to find Poison Ivy at the top. But he found Solomon Grundy too! Were you surprised that the two villains were there? Why or why not?

2. Batman wasn't sure about trusting Poison Ivy and working with her. Why? What would you have done?

3. The Dark Knight didn't fight Solomon Grundy head-on. He snuck through the leafy building to get the captives out one by one. Do you think this was a good or bad choice? Use examples from the story to explain your answer.

WRITE ABOUT IT

1. Batman uses his smarts and gadgets to take down villains. Make a list of three devices he used during the story. Then write a paragraph arguing which one you think is the most useful.

2. Imagine you are Gregory Gild or Mariah Vega. Write the story of how you were snatched away. Then tell the tale of how you were rescued by a Super Hero!

3. Fairy tales are often told and retold over many generations, and the details can change depending on who tells them. Write your version of the "Jack and the Beanstalk" story. You can change a lot or a little. But make it your own!

The Author

Sarah Hines Stephens lives a fairy tale life in Oakland, California, with her two magical kids, a pair of charming dogs, and a prince of a husband. If she could pick a superpower, it would definitely be flight so she could zoom all over the world having adventures, trying out new foods, and visiting far-flung friends and family. Sarah has written over one hundred books for kids about all kinds of crazy characters—none of whom hold a candle to the wacky cast she loves and lives with.

The Illustrators

Agnes Garbowska is an artist who has worked with many major book publishers, illustrating such brands as DC Super Hero Girls, Teen Titans Go!, My Little Pony, and Care Bears. She was born in Poland and came to Canada at a young age. Being an only child, she escaped into a world of books, cartoons, and comics. She currently lives in the United States and enjoys sharing her office with her two little dogs.

Sil Brys is a colorist and graphic designer. She has worked on many comics and children's books, having had fun coloring stories for Teen Titans Go!, Scooby-Doo, Tom & Jerry, Looney Tunes, DC Super Hero Girls, Care Bears, and more. She lives in a small village in Argentina, where her home is also her office. She loves to create there, surrounded by forests, mountains, and a lot of books.